Not Quite Changed

Emily Martha Sorensen

Also by Emily Martha Sorensen

Wicked Witches of Restva:
Black Magic Academy
White Magic Academy

The End in the Beginning:
The Keeper and the Rulership
The Fires of the Rulership
The Magic or the Rulership

Fairy Senses:
Fairy Eyeglasses
Fairy Compass
Fairy Earmuffs
Fairy Barometer
Fairy Pox
Fairy Slippers
Fairy Lunchbox
Fairy Icepack
Fairy Stopwatch
Fairy Toothbrush
Fairy Perfume
Fairy Crown

Dragon Eggs:
Dragon's Egg
Dragon's Hope
Dragon's First Christmas
Dragon's Fire
Dragon's Song
Dragon's First Valentine

Comics:
A Magical Roommate
To Prevent World Peace

The Numbers Just Keep
Getting Bigger:
Twenty-Four Potential
Children of Prophecy

Trilogy of a Teenage Werevulture:
Trials of a Teenage Werevulture
Trifles of a Teenage Werevulture

Weredodo Cozy Mysteries:
Weredodo Sleuth

The Virgo Curse:
Not Quite a Curse
Not Quite a Blessing

Magical Mayhem:
To Prevent World Peace
To Prevent Chic Costumes
To Prevent Clear Paths
To Prevent Smart Choices
To Prevent Warm Welcomes
To Prevent Cute Mascots
To Prevent First Place (prologue)
To Prevent Fresh Starts
To Prevent New Allies
To Prevent Best Friends
To Prevent Good Luck

Short Story Collections:
Worlds of Wonder
Magic and Mischief
Tales of Tie-Ins

Picture Books:
Tabby, Tabby, Burning Bright

http://www.emilymarthasorensen.com

To all the authors of shoujo manga
who have given me
loads of enjoyment over the years.

You know what inspired this book.

Chapter 1
Not Quite Fine

"Queen Lucy's adding to her harem again, I see," Carrie said snidely.

Lucy glanced uncomfortably over to the side. Was Tom . . .? Yep. Natasia's older brother was watching her from behind the grill with an admiring look on his face. She'd always vaguely thought he was cute, and apparently her power had activated on him.

"Lucy can't help it if she's hotter than the food he's cooking," Pablo teased, plopping his arm around her shoulders.

"Ouch!" Lucy mock-squealed, jumping away. "You're even hotter than I am!"

"If you want to make a date with him, I can take a turn at the grill so you can talk to him," George said seriously.

"No!" Carrie snapped. "This is Natasia's birthday party! Don't you dare make it all about you, Lucy. You already have two dates going on right now!"

Lucy laughed sheepishly. Yeahhh, she'd sort of brought two dates to Natasia's backyard birthday barbecue. But there was a reason for it!

Not that she could tell anyone that reason.

The reason was that, wellllllll, she'd made a rule that she couldn't go out with the same guy more often than once every third date. That was because she didn't dare start going out with any one guy exclusively. It was what the curse wanted her to do.

And, meanwhile, she'd had a date with Pablo only last night. But Natasia had invited Pablo to the party herself because he got along so well with all of their group, and Pablo was so fun that Lucy knew it would turn into a date if she didn't bring somebody else to be her technical date for the event, soooooooooo . . . she'd invited George.

The other options would have been Jonas or Billy, guys she liked almost as much as George. But both of them got annoyed whenever she flirted with other guys while on dates with them, and she couldn't *not* flirt with Pablo when he was nearby, so yeah, she'd brought George.

"Don't go to the grill," Lucy told George with a teasing smile. "I like where you are right now."

George smiled and stroked her hand that was near him.

Pablo's arm around Lucy's shoulder tightened, and he scooted possessively closer. It seemed that while George was perfectly comfortable sharing her with Pablo, the reverse was not true.

"Now taking bets on who Lucy picks as a steady boyfriend!" Matilda stage-whispered from the other end of the table. "Ten bucks on George because he's the cutest!"

"Fifteen on Jonas because she's known him the longest," Jezza shot back.

"Twenty on Pablo because I think she likes him the best," Natasia grinned.

"Thirty on no one," Carrie smirked. "Queen Lucy is incapable of monogamy."

"You guyyyyyyys!" Lucy exclaimed.

"I'll place a bet on myself, if that's allowed!" Pablo called.

"Oooooh!" Jezza and Matilda giggled.

"I'm going to chop vegetables for the veggie platter!" Lucy informed them, shoving back her chair. "Nobody follow me!"

Not Quite Fine

Laughter rolled across the group as she stormed off.

It's not that I'm incapable of monogamy! Lucy thought angrily, stomping up the stairs of the deck in order to reach the kitchen. *In fact, if I could pick Pab— one of the guys I like best, I would. But I can't! It would make the curse kill me faster!*

If she picked Billy because they had the exact same taste in movies, or Jonas because she'd had a crush on him as a kid and he still had the same wickedly sarcastic sense of humor, or George because he was the nicest guy she'd ever met, or Pablo because he was, well, duh, *Pablo,* it would mean letting the curse win. And she didn't want to give the curse any victories.

It wasn't like any of those guys were perfect, either. She'd only met Billy two weeks ago, so even though they got along great, she didn't know him that well. Jonas's jokes could be cruel and cutting. George's complete lack of jealousy got on her nerves. And Pablo . . .

Well, okay, Pablo *was* pretty much perfect. But his family was annoying.

Just last night, his unbelievable aunt had followed them to a restaurant to take pictures of one of their dates to put into their "future wedding scrapbook."

Granted, the way he'd yelled at her in Spanish about keeping her nose out of his business had been awesome.

And it still made her giggle to remember one of the things he'd yelled in Spanish, which she was sure he didn't realize she'd understood: *"Yes, I'd love it if she wants to marry me someday, but if that happens, it'll be on our timing and not yours, and I'll thank you to not scare her away!"*

He was so, so, *SO* great. But . . . that didn't mean she could afford to choose him.

Smile dropping from her face, Lucy shoved open the screen door and found Natasia's boyfriend chopping up celery.

"Hi, Sean," Lucy said, waving. "Can I help?"

"Nah, there's only one cutting board."

She looked down at the veggie platter. "Can I put the ranch dressing on there?"

He gestured at the refrigerator. "Sure."

Lucy squeezed too hard, and way too much ranch dressing splatted into the center. The excess ran over into the baby carrots. She grabbed a baby carrot and tried to shove the excess back into the middle as it kept pouring back.

She glanced sheepishly over at Sean, only to see that he was still methodically cutting tomato wedges with his back turned to her. He clearly hadn't noticed her minor misadventure with the ranch dressing, which meant he hadn't turned around to look at her once.

Chop. Chop. Chop. Chop. He kept on going without missing a beat.

Lucy frowned, puzzled. Sean was a weird mystery. He was the only guy she found attractive that she'd never caught trying to sneak glances at her. That was a good thing, since he was her friend Natasia's boyfriend, but she'd never been able to figure out why.

"How are you immune?" Lucy blurted out.

Sean looked up, clearly puzzled. "To what?"

Lucy wanted to bite her tongue. None of her friends knew about the curse, and she wanted to keep it that way.

On the other hand, she *did* want the answer to that question. As far as she knew, the only way for her power to not activate was for her to not find a guy attractive.

"Let's say there's such a thing as love potions," Lucy hedged. That was far enough away from the truth that the curse would let her say it.

"Okay?" Sean looked clearly mystified.

"Let's say it splashed on somebody, and it was an accident, and it couldn't be turned off."

"Okay . . .?"

"And let's say it happened to me." Lucy took a deep breath. *"How are you immune?"*

Sean stared at her for a long moment.

"I'm not," he said, shrugging.

Lucy stared at him. *"What?"*

He looked a bit embarrassed. "I assume you're talking about the way you suddenly got really hot a few months ago, and every guy at school noticed? I dunno what it is, since you look the same as ever, but I get why the other guys are always staring at you. I just don't care. Natasia's the only girl who matters."

Lucy's mouth opened in astonishment. That possibility had never occurred to her.

So the curse isn't everything? They still have a choice?!

That was good news. No, it was great news. No, it was amazing!

"You're a great guy," she said, managing to keep her voice level instead of showing off her jubilation. "I'm glad Natasia has you."

"Me, too!" He glanced back at her with a grin.

Lucy picked up the veggie platter and walked over, moving tomato wedges from the chopping board as he prepared more.

She breathed a sigh of contentment. This meant she never had to worry that she'd steal Sean, because Sean wouldn't be stolen. He'd chosen Natasia, even with magic trying to tempt him away. That was the best thing ever.

Her hand hovered over the platter, and she swallowed a lump in her throat.

But I'll never have what they have, will I?

Because none of the guys she was currently dating had ever been given the opportunity to choose her. Not really. None of them knew that their feelings were probably magically induced.

Xander's curse had been a dealbreaker for Lucy. Lucy's curse might be a dealbreaker for any of them. So they deserved the chance to hear the truth and say "no."

Lucy took a deep, shaky breath.

That doesn't matter, she tried to convince herself. *As long as no relationship ever gets serious enough that I HAVE to tell the guy everything, it's fine to keep it a secret. It is!*

But the more she thought about it, the more it bothered her.

Chapter 2
Not Quite Long

"

—— Visit him," Lucy's mom was saying as she arrived back home from the birthday party a few hours later. "Oh, Lucy! I have bad news! Aaron fell and broke his hip!"

"Aaron Ahlstrom?" Lucy hazarded. That was the football player at school that Carrie was currently crushing on. She'd spent a solid fifteen minutes of the barbecue talking about him.

"Aaron Watson!" her mother said impatiently. "The Aries!"

Ohhh, him. The nice old guy. Lucy flinched a little. *I hope nobody calls me "the Virgo." I hate that Mom thinks it's okay to refer to people by their curses.*

"I'm sure it was painful," Lucy's mom nodded, misinterpreting her grimace. "We're going to go see him at the hospital. You got home just in time. You can come with us."

"Do I have to?" Lucy blurted out.

The dangerous look in her mother's eyes told Lucy that this had been the wrong thing to say.

"I mean, do I have to go with you?" Lucy amended quickly. "I want to go by myself. It'll be more personal that way."

"Oh." Her mother's expression softened. "I suppose so. You can borrow the car after we get back."

"Perfect," Lucy said, giving a cheerful thumbs-up.

It was all she could do to keep from grumbling inside as she went up the stairs to her room, though.

It wasn't that she didn't care about the old man. Breaking a hip sounded awful. But she didn't actually know him that well, and if she were the one in the hospital and maybe doped up on pain medication, she wouldn't want a bunch of almost-strangers coming to visit her. She'd want them to leave her alone.

On top of that, she'd just come home from a long afternoon of trying to seem cheerful and normal, and she wanted to hide in her room for awhile away from people.

Are Virgos introverts? she wondered, struck by the terrible thought at the top of the stairs. *This could be the curse trying to affect me.*

"Wait!" Lucy called, charging back down the stairs. "I changed my mind! I think it'd be better if we all visit him together. Less chance we'll tire him out or something."

"That's a good idea," her mother said approvingly. "Harry! Are you ready?"

"I don't see why we have to go in the first place," Lucy's dad grumbled, coming in from the living room with a well-worn copy of *The Art of War* in his hand. It was his idea of some relaxing light reading. "We barely know the man."

Lucy hid a giggle behind her hand.

"Harry," her mom said in a reproving tone, "it's important to show respect and solidarity."

"No, it's important for me to enjoy my day off."

Lucy felt significantly more cheered as they tromped to the car. It helped to know her father felt the same way she did.

She played a cellphone game during the drive there, and her father kept reading his book.

When they arrived at the hospital, they went to the right floor, checked in at the desk, were told Aaron's room number, and all headed there together.

Lucy crossed her fingers, hoping the old man would be asleep and they wouldn't have to make stiltedly awkward conversation, but no such luck. He was sitting up, wide awake, and in a friendly mood.

"Harry! Iris! Lucy!" he said, smiling and turning off the TV. "How good of you to come!"

"We heard about your hip," Lucy's mother said with concern, walking over to the bed and sitting in the chair beside it. "How are you doing?"

Aaron shrugged. "I can't say I'm exactly good, but . . . I'm all right. How are you doing?"

"Oh, we're fine," Lucy's mom said, waving her hand. "Is there anything we can do for you?"

"No, I'm fine, fine. Tell me what's up with you."

"We're not important right now. You are. Are you hurting? Are they giving you everything you need?"

"Mom," Lucy cut in, "he's obviously trying to say, 'Please don't feel sorry for me, because it makes me feel like an invalid.'"

Lucy's dad coughed in a way that was clearly trying to hide a laugh.

Her mother glanced back at both of them, glaring.

Aaron's lips twitched. "Well . . . she's not wrong. I'd rather be distracted from my own life right now. So please. Tell me how things are going with you."

Lucy's mother frowned, but she eventually launched into a long description of the way she had been tracking Lucy's behavior over the last few months and the worrisome places she thought she had seen hints of changes.

Aaron responded to the topic with evident interest, and they talked about it for awhile, which Lucy found intensely boring and intensely embarrassing.

She glanced over at her father with agonized eyes.

"Let's go get Aaron a snack from the vending machine," he suggested, removing his finger from his book and tucking it into his pocket. He had been sneaking glances at it every few seconds. "Aaron, is there anything you're not allowed to eat?"

Not Quite Long

"Oh, I probably shouldn't eat candy, but I'd love a Snickers."

"Good to know." Her dad gestured with his head. "C'mon, Lucy. Let's go get him something."

Lucy followed him out of the room with relief.

Once they were out of earshot, she whispered furiously, "Why is Mom so . . . so . . ."

"She cares about people," Lucy's father said firmly, in a tone that made it clear he wasn't going to listen to any badmouthing. "That's why she's trying so hard to track your behavior. I know you don't like it, but it could be important to keep you alive longer."

Lucy sighed heavily. She knew that. She *knew* that, but she still hated it.

"Hey," her dad said, putting his arm around her shoulders, "I'll buy you something, too. What are you in the mood for?"

Not being in a hospital, Lucy thought, but that didn't seem like the right answer. "Peanut butter M&Ms," she said.

They found a cluster of vending machines, including one with Snickers bars, but none with peanut butter M&Ms.

"No problem," her dad said. "I'm sure there are a bunch of vending machines on every floor. Let's check out all of them."

Lucy was glad for the excuse to stay out of the room as long as possible, so they went on a long treasure hunt around the hospital until they found a vending machine with Reese's Pieces, which she determined were close enough.

They headed back up to Aaron's floor and came in with the Snickers bar for him. Lucy's mother, still engaged in conversation with the old man, didn't notice them enter until Aaron interrupted her to wave and say hi.

"Here's a Snickers," Lucy's dad said, walking over and placing it on the bed beside Aaron.

"Thank you," the old man said with a smile. "That's very kind of you. Iris, may I talk with Lucy for a few minutes?"

Lucy's mother nodded, as if this was something they had discussed earlier, and took her husband's hand and guided him out of the room without comment. Their footsteps faded down the hallway.

Lucy stared at the brown-skinned old man, mystified. Why did Aaron want to talk to her? Was he going to tell her to pay more attention to her mother's stupid spreadsheet?

He didn't say anything at first. He just peeled the candy bar and took a bite, chewing it slowly as if he was savoring it.

Lucy frowned, puzzled and wondering why she was here.

At last, Aaron swallowed and set the rest aside.

"I'm not going to live much longer, Lucy," he said.

Her eyes widened. "What? Are you sure?!"

He smiled softly. "Well, the odds of a senior citizen living longer than a year after breaking a hip are fifty percent. I'm not going to beat those odds."

"You could," Lucy said hotly. "That's fifty percent. Half do!"

"But I don't want to," Aaron said quietly. "I'm content with the life I've had, and I'm not eager to spend another ten years losing myself to my condition, especially given the ability it grants me. Do you understand?"

"No!" Lucy said heatedly. "I *don't* understand!"

"Think about what I can do, Lucy."

Lucy frowned. "You can persuade people to do things, right?"

"Yes. Now think about that in conjunction with the personality I'm inevitably going to be stuck with by the end of my life, unless I pass away of natural causes long before then."

Lucy stared at him in puzzlement.

Aaron waited patiently, his hands on his lap.

Lucy pulled out her phone and looked up *Aries personality traits*. Google found what she was looking for immediately.

"Passionate. Motivated. A confident leader. Blindly optimistic. Always convinced that they're right. Competitive. Impulsive. Selfish. Annoyed by details and nuances. Doesn't think things through."

Her mouth went dry.

Chapter 3
Not Quite Safe

Even though she didn't say anything, Aaron seemed to know what she was thinking just by the look on her face. He chuckled.

"Yes. I see you've realized."

You've got a mind-control power! Lucy wanted to yell, but couldn't say. *And you're going to turn into someone who thinks they're always right and who wants to be in charge of everybody they meet!*

Aaron picked up his candy bar, peeled back the wrapper a bit farther, and took another bite. He chewed and swallowed. "As you might guess, I don't think it would be particularly safe for the world for me to live much longer."

"But — you can't — I mean, you shouldn't —" Lucy wasn't quite sure what she was fumbling to say. She just knew that it sounded way too much like he was planning to commit suicide.

"I'm not going to end my life deliberately," he said calmly. "For one thing, every day I live is another day my granddaughter isn't affected. I'd rather she have as much time unaffected by this situation as possible."

Lucy breathed a sigh of relief.

"But I've signed a do-not-resuscitate order," Aaron told her. "And I had a mild heart attack last year. I won't take my own life, but I won't take steps to prolong it if my time comes, either. I see breaking my hip as a sign that I should prepare to die soon."

Tears rose in the corners of Lucy's eyes. "That's stupid!"

"You're young," Aaron retorted. "You don't know what it's like to be old, bored, tired of life, and ready to see if there's something else afterwards."

"Then why are you telling me this?!" Lucy exclaimed. "If I can't understand, what's the *point?*"

Aaron said nothing at first, but took another bite of his Snickers bar. It was almost gone now. He chewed and swallowed for what seemed like a really long time. Then, at last, he spoke.

"My granddaughter is only seven years old. Her name is Ellen, and her family's going to be moving here in anticipation of what happens to her after I die."

She was his heir, in other words. That was one of the words cursed people never seemed to be able to say.

"I want you to look after her," Aaron continued. "She's always wanted a big sister, and I think she'd look up to you."

Lucy's mouth opened. "Me?!"

"Yes. When I'm gone and she's part of the . . . group, I want you to make sure she's included and happy. She'll be the only child among all of you, and I suspect that will make her unhappy and unlikely to listen to advice from a bunch of strangers, especially after just barely having been forced to move to a new city. Her parents haven't explained any of this to her yet. If you take her under your wing, I think that will help her."

Lucy gulped. "But I don't know how to be an older sister."

She knew how to be a *younger* sister, but ever since Lila had gone away to college, she'd mostly felt like an only child, and she enjoyed it. She and Lila got along much better when they only talked on the phone, instead of squabbling over who had stolen whose pants from whose closet yesterday.

Never mind that the pants thief was usually Lucy.

Not Quite Safe

"But you do know how to be friendly and engaging," Aaron countered. "Your mother says you make friends easily, and you certainly seem to have a lot of them. I'm not saying that you have to treat her as if she's blood-related, but a little bit of making sure to single her out and pay attention to her and be nice to her will go a long way."

Lucy was silent. It wasn't too much to ask, and it wasn't like it would make her Virgo curse worse. Making friends easily was something she did naturally. But it was uncomfortable to have someone asking her to be friends with someone else she'd never met. What if the girl was a royal brat? What if they had nothing in common and just didn't get along?

"I guess I can try," Lucy hedged.

Then a horrible realization crawled up the back of her neck.

"You didn't just convince me, did you?!" she gasped, her whole body stiffening.

Aaron sighed heavily. "No, Lucy. If I had, you wouldn't have been able to consider the possibility. You would trust me implicitly."

Scariest. Power. Ever. Lucy shuddered.

Aaron finished off the last bite of his candy bar. He crumpled the wrapper in his hand and set it on the table beside the bed. "Thank you, Lucy. Knowing that someone will be watching over her eases my mind. If I can do anything to help you, please let me know."

"You're welcome. I'll keep that in mind," Lucy said to be polite. Honestly, she couldn't see what an old man with a broken hip and a terrifying power could do to help anybody. But he was nice, so she wouldn't hurt his feelings by saying so.

"I mean it," Aaron said, reaching out and squeezing her hand. His wrinkled skin was soft and loose, like melted chocolate. "If I can do anything, let me know."

"Okay, I will, I promise," Lucy said uncomfortably, extracting her hand.

She glanced over her shoulder. *When is Mom coming back?*

In the end, it took ten more minutes for her parents to return, leaving her and Aaron in uncomfortable silence for awhile.

Her mother said goodbye to the old man, giving him a gentle hug without squeezing him too tightly, and Lucy's father waved goodbye with a poorly disguised expression of relief.

In the car, Lucy's mom glanced back from the driver's seat before backing out, and said, "Well? Did you agree to help his granddaughter?"

Of course Mom had known what Aaron wanted to ask her. "Yeah," Lucy said. "She sounds nice. I hope she is."

"That's good." Lucy's mom smiled. "I'm sure you would have appreciated an older sister figure if you'd inherited your curse at her age."

I already have an older sister figure, and she's Lila. "I guess," Lucy shrugged.

"Personally, I don't see much point in asking Lucy to befriend a stranger she's never met," her father opined. "Not to mention one that's nine years younger. I don't think they'll have that much in common."

"Harry!" her mom said in annoyance.

Personally, Lucy was inclined to agree, but she knew better than to take sides when her parents were arguing. Whenever she did, the parent she sided with would jump to the other's side, and then she'd turn into the one they were annoyed with.

So she just smiled to herself and started a game on her phone. She glanced up a minute later to see her father tapping his finger on a paragraph thoughtfully.

That had better not be an idea about how to embarrass me in front of tonight's date, Dad! Lucy thought indignantly.

She had a first date tonight. Yet another one. She really ought to start turning those guys down. But without a steady boyfriend as an excuse, she couldn't do that without hurting their feelings.

And, well, she couldn't have a steady boyfriend, because that would be bad.

Stupid curse.

The more she thought about her conversation with Aaron, though, the more it disturbed her. Not the favor, but the fact that he wanted to die soon to protect the world from his power.

Not Quite Safe

He could change minds.
She could change hearts.
He was warning people that his power existed. She wasn't.
Lucy bit her lip uncomfortably. *Do I need to start?*

Chapter 4
Not Quite Right

"Please make an exception for me," the guy in front of her pleaded.

Lucy groaned in exasperation. Tonight's first date, Andrew, would not be getting a second. But he was trying to insist on her scheduling one on the front step of her house before they parted ways anyway. What a loser.

"No," Lucy said firmly. "I don't make dates more than a week in advance, and I'm busy the rest of this week. Sorry."

"Please!" Andrew exclaimed.

Lucy pursed her lips and stared intently at his face, looking for any flaws. None stood out, which was probably why he was still attracted to her. It was hard to make herself stop liking a guy who was that good-looking.

But she'd better do it, because he was getting on her nerves. Maybe she could focus on his voice, which was now sounding distinctly whiny. Or the fact that he seemed to be clumsy.

Boys who beg for dates after spilling soda all over my lap are not attractive, Lucy told herself firmly.

"Sorry," she said, pulling her key out of her pocket to open the door.

Andrew lunged forward and tried to kiss her. Lucy yelped and jabbed her hand out to protect herself. Her key slashed the side of his face.

"Oww!" Andrew shouted, clutching his cheek. "What was that for?!"

"I don't kiss on the first date, and certainly not guys who don't bother to ask first!" Lucy yelled back. "Why would you think that's okay?!"

"But I have to! My friend bet me fifty dollars I couldn't get you to kiss me!"

Lucy stared at him incredulously. Then she spun around, jammed her key in the lock, flung the door open, stalked in, and slammed the door in his face.

"Sounds like a successful date," her father called gleefully from the living room, where he was watching a football game on TV and sipping a cup of chamomile tea.

"Such! A! Nightmare!" Lucy exclaimed, storming over to the living room. "Why do first dates so often stink?"

"Because you go on way too many of them," her father said smugly, muting the television set.

Lucy flopped into a chair, unwilling to admit she agreed. "So what's the solution?"

Her father gave her a lazy smile. "Well, there's always —"

"I'm not going to quit going out on *all* dates, Dad!"

He guffawed.

"Of course, I'm sure it didn't help that you told him if he proved to have more hands than two, you'd be happy to relieve him of the extras," Lucy added, folding her arms.

"Just protecting my little girl," he said with a grin.

Lucy flopped back against the couch, sighing. "I wish I could stop going on first dates, but I can't do that without making it look like I'm about to choose a boyfriend to commit to, y'know? And I don't want to raise P— um, anyone's hopes."

"So why don't you just choose a boyfriend to commit to?"

Lucy stared at him. This, from her overprotective dad? "What?"

"It seems to me that that's the obvious solution. If it doesn't work out, you could dump that boy and choose another."

"But I can't do that!" Lucy exclaimed.

"Why not?" He looked puzzled.

"Because! Because I think that's what the thing-I-can't-say wants me to do!"

Her father blinked. "You think the curse cares if you have a boyfriend?"

"Yes!" Lucy exclaimed. "I think the whole point of the thing-I-can-do is to make me sick of having tons of guys after me and want to settle down with just one, which is totally the kind of thing a person with my birthdate should supposedly be doing!"

Lucy's father opened his mouth, as if he were about to say something. Then he shut it again, looking puzzled.

"Okay, setting aside the fact that my sister stayed single for her whole life, and still died of the Virgo curse," he said at last, "why would you think it's a good idea to not do things you want to do just because the curse wants you to do them?"

"Because I don't want to die!"

"Yes, I approve of that goal." Her father nodded. "But you might want to consider this: if you don't want to be single for the rest of your life, then the sooner you find a relationship you want to stay in, the better a chance you have of finding someone who likes you, and not Virgo."

Lucy swallowed. That thought had never occurred to her. "But if it makes me die sooner —"

"If you'd stayed to listen to any of Steven's advice at the last meeting," her father said with a hint of exasperation, "you'd know that permanently single people tend to die more quickly of the curses than people in a relationship. His theory is that having someone who cares even more than you do about you staying alive and staying yourself is very helpful."

Lucy swallowed. Well, now that he made it seem like her getting a boyfriend was her best chance to stay alive longer, she paradoxically didn't want one. That sounded scary.

Not Quite Right

"But you'd hate that," Lucy argued. "You hate it when I go out on dates!"

"No, I hate the endless parade of strange boys showing up at our house that I don't trust with my daughter." He snorted. "At this point, seeing you settle down with one boy I know moderately well and don't mind would be a relief."

Lucy was starting to feel panicked. Did he mean she had to pick somebody? She wasn't ready to pick somebody! If she did, she'd have to break a bunch of other guys' hearts, and she didn't want to hurt anyone!

Besides, what if she got dumped and had no backup plans that she could live with waiting for her?!

"Of course, there's no rush," her dad said. "If you'd rather take a break from boys until college, for instance, that would be fine."

Until college?! "Daaaaaaaaaad!" Lucy exclaimed.

Her father sipped his probably-now-cold chamomile tea and grinned.

"I'll figure it out myself," Lucy fumed, hopping up to her feet. "Thanks for nothing, Dad."

"You're welcome for nothing, Lucy."

"I can't believe you're trying to convince me to get a boyfriend! I don't want a boyfriend! You're crazy!"

"Excellent. Nothing would make me more ecstatic than you not dating until you're old enough to get married."

"But that doesn't mean I *won't* get one!" Lucy flared.

"Then I suppose I'll tolerate that."

"Now you're just assuming I *will!* Don't try to make decisions for me! Ugh!"

Her father looked highly amused. "So you have the opposite opinion of whatever I say? Fascinating. In that case, I'd love to see you go out with hundreds of boys forever."

Lucy stamped her foot. "Stop making fun of me!"

"Then don't make it so easy."

"I don't want to dump any of the guys I like!" Lucy cried. "It'll hurt their feelings!"

"Leading 'em on will just hurt them worse."

Lucy hesitated. "So you're saying maybe I should narrow it down to only guys I might consider dating exclusively?" she asked in a small voice.

"Oh, no," her father said. "I'm saying nothing of the sort. Not when it seems to be opposite day."

Lucy snorted and turned to stomp out of the room.

"Lucy?" her father called after her.

"Yeah?" she asked saucily.

"Not the one with the nose ring, okay?"

"Dad, I dumped him two months ago!"

"Oh, good." Her father sounded pleased.

Chapter 5
Not Quite Fair

Zipping through a rack of jeans to see if she could find a pair that was both cute and fit her during this week's massive sale, Lucy was startled to hear a familiar voice off to the side.

"Aw, Mom, c'mon. Can't we just buy the first one?"

"No, you're going to try on all five."

There was a disgusted groan and the sound of footsteps stomping off.

Lucy ducked below the rack she was examining and peeked around the side, checking to see if it was the person she'd thought. Yep, that was Caleb's retreating back.

Phooey. That made her shopping trip much less relaxing.

Lucy contemplated whether she should hurry off before he noticed her, or whether she should just pretend he wasn't there and keep looking through jeans she might want to buy.

Avarice won out. It wasn't her fault that Caleb insisted on making it awkward whenever they ran into each other, and she had sixty dollars of birthday money she wanted to spend on new jeans today.

She turned her back to the men's changing rooms, hoping he wouldn't recognize her from behind when he came out, and went back to browsing.

Ooh, those jeans with the flower pockets were cute! And they were a good price, too. The size was a little too big, though. Did they have a pair in her size? She slid her way through a bunch of identical ones, looking for a pair that was the right size so she could try them on.

"Hey, look, they fit," Caleb's voice said from behind her. "Just like I said they would. Now can we buy these and go?"

"Nuh uh," said a bossy woman's voice. "You want me to pay for your clothes, I get the privilege of approving them. Now turn around so I can see how they look from the back."

Caleb groaned loudly.

Lucy stifled a giggle with her hand. Their conversation was reminding her of going back-to-school shopping with her mom when she was a kid. But seeing as Caleb was her age, hearing him whine like an elementary schooler was hilarious.

"Okay, good," the woman's voice said. "Those are a maybe. Now try on the next pair."

There was a loud exhale, clearly meant to be a less-than-subtle complaint, then the sound of footsteps treading away again.

Lucy couldn't resist. She turned around and asked the woman, "Is he always such a baby about clothes shopping?"

"A total infant," the woman said, shaking her head. She had dark brown skin, a bald head, and enormous earrings that swung as her head moved. "I wish my daughter was the one who needed new clothes. Maybe then this would be fun, rather than an ordeal."

"Or it'd be *more* of an ordeal, because she'd be begging you to buy her extra stuff every two minutes," Lucy said impishly. She and her sister tended to do that to their mom whenever they went shopping together. It drove their mom nuts.

"Good point," the woman said. "I guess my son will do. I'm Tammy. What's your name?"

"Lucy," Lucy said.

"Cool." Tammy surveyed her. "How old are you?"

"Sixteen."

"Perfect. My son's age. You can give your opinions on how the jeans look on him. I don't really have much perspective on whether he looks attractive to a teenage girl or not."

Lucy stifled a hysterical giggle behind her hand. "Um, I don't think Caleb wants my opinion."

"Why not?"

Caleb emerged from the dressing room, strode over with a bored-to-death look on his face, and then stopped abruptly. "*You!*" he shouted.

"Hi, Caleb," Lucy said sheepishly. She knew she shouldn't have started a conversation with his mom, but honestly, how was she supposed to have resisted?

"You know each other?" Tammy asked, looking confused.

"She's the one with the making-people-fall-in-love-with-her power!" Caleb shouted.

Lucy glanced around in alarm, hoping nobody she knew was nearby and listening in. Fortunately, none of her friends or other people in school were in sight.

"Oh, really?" Tammy asked with interest. "I've heard a lot about you from Steven. What's that power like? Is it fun?"

"No, it's awful!" Lucy blurted out. "I never know if anyone *actually* likes me, and the only two guys who've known about it have rejected me because I had it!"

Technically that wasn't totally true. Caleb had done that, but she'd rejected Xander, not the other way around.

Still, he definitely hadn't come back.

Which didn't hurt or anything. Really, it didn't. It was just, well, maybe part of her had hoped he'd fallen in love with her for real and would come back saying that he didn't care about the danger to himself; he just wanted her. The fact that he had done the exact opposite . . .

. . . didn't hurt at all. Really, it didn't.

Besides, she liked Pablo way more anyway. He was just as fun as Xander, and he didn't have that nasty temper. Plus, his personality was his own.

But he also didn't know about the curse. She didn't know how he'd react to finding out what her power did. And when she imagined Pablo sneering at her in that cold, contemptuous way Xander had right before leaving, she wanted to cry.

It would be bad enough if he indignantly rejected her, like Caleb had. But contempt . . . she couldn't stand it if he looked at her with contempt. She just couldn't.

And what if all her backup plans did the same thing?

Caleb was folding his arms and looking utterly unsympathetic.

"Sounds to me like the only way to find out is to tell them," Tammy said.

"Yeah, at the start, so they won't feel tricked and deceived," Caleb said acidly.

Tammy flicked him hard in the arm.

"Ow!" he complained, grabbing the spot.

"Ignore my son's denseness. Of course you can't tell them the truth from the start," Tammy said briskly. "It's a question of privacy, isn't it? You don't want to be the gossip of the entire school."

Lucy swallowed and nodded.

"So pick a set amount of time in which you'll either break up with a guy or trust him enough to tell him the truth. One or the other. That's what Steven did. He told me about being the heir to a curse on our sixth date. Kind of a shocker, let me tell you."

Lucy bit her lower lip. *But . . . I mean . . . obviously I trust Pablo and George and Jonas and Billy to not tell anyone by now. I just don't trust any of them to not break up with me!*

Lucy cringed. Now that she'd put it into words, that seemed disgustingly selfish.

"Do I have to pick a set amount of time?" she hedged.

"Absolutely," Tammy said. "If you don't, you'll keep making excuses to put it off long after the point where you could have done it, and that isn't quite fair. Don't you think?"

Bingo. Lucy felt a little queasy.

"But I *can't* tell them the whole truth," Lucy argued, knowing she was grasping at straws. "That's how it works. I can't explain anything directly."

Not Quite Fair

"Then get somebody else to do it," Tammy shrugged.

"I'll do it!" Caleb said with a grin. He punched a fist into his hand. "Let me at 'em."

"I'd rather die," Lucy retorted.

Caleb snickered. "C'mon. I'll only embarrass you *half* as badly as you humiliated me."

"I didn't do it on purpose! And don't you have jeans to try on?"

"Good point," Tammy said, pointing to the changing room. "Let's see you in the next pair."

"They're all exactly the same," Caleb grumbled. But he left.

Lucy sighed and turned to leave.

"Hey. It's not as bad as you think," Tammy called after her. "Some people are okay with dealing with hard things."

"Easy for you to say," Lucy said angrily, wiping the edge of her eyes to get rid of wetness that was totally not forming there. "You don't have what I've got."

"Yeah, I'm just in the middle of treatment for breast cancer," Tammy said sarcastically. "You think the threat of dying maybe a decade from now is bad? Big whoop-de-freaking-doo."

Lucy swallowed. She had somehow managed to forget that there were problems that weren't supernatural that were every bit as bad as a curse.

"Thanks for your advice," she said almost inaudibly, and then hightailed it out of there.

Chapter 6
Not Quite Brave

Justifications and excuses weren't any use, so Lucy vowed that she would tell Billy the truth on their date the next night.

He was the perfect choice to tell first. He was on the list of guys she might consider as a possible boyfriend, but he was at the bottom of the list. That meant if he rejected her, or if he did something horrible like betray her trust and turn her curse into a rumor at school, she'd be able to handle it.

Meanwhile, if everything went well, she'd be all the more prepared to tell the truth to Jonas. Or George. Or Pablo.

Her pulse accelerated in panic.

No, not Pablo. Not him. Not yet. She had to save him for last. He was the one she was most afraid would reject her. His family was so controlling and pushy. She was certain he'd hate the idea of her curse doing the same thing to him, only more insidiously.

But maybe . . . if the other boys she liked best were all okay with it . . . he'd turn out to be, too.

Lucy took a deep breath, pulled her hair back, changed her clothes, and sprayed her wrist with her favorite perfume.

Not Quite Brave

There. Now she was all ready for tonight's date.

Oh, wait! Billy's allergic to perfume! She dashed to the sink in the upstairs bathroom to scrub it off.

When Billy arrived, she felt jumpy, and her voice sounded too loud whenever she answered a question. He didn't seem to notice, though, and soon they were in a movie theater, sharing a bucket of popcorn.

Well, I can't tell him now, Lucy told herself, relaxing back into her seat. *I'll have to wait till the movie's over.*

Once the movie was over, they drove back, chatting about the scenes they'd enjoyed most and the moments they'd thought were stupid. As always, they had the same opinion on everything in the movie. That was what Lucy liked about him.

Then they were back at the door, and Lucy realized that she hadn't told him anything important yet, or even tried to bring up the subject.

"Billy," Lucy began, pleating her hands nervously. "There's, um, there's something you ought to know."

"Huh?" He cocked his head to the side.

Lucy swallowed. Her heart pounded. Even the vaguest words that the curse would allow her to say stuck in her mouth.

"Never mind!" Lucy cried, and grabbed the doorknob. She flung the door open, ran a step inside, and then turned back and gave Billy a hurried kiss on the cheek. "You're a great guy, Billy. Thanks for being so fun to hang out with."

"You're welcome," Billy beamed, giving her a thumbs-up.

Lucy shut the door and leaned against it, shoulders heaving.

I'm a coward, she thought, filled with self-recrimination and despair. *If I can't tell Billy, how can I ever tell anybody?*

If only there were some way to become brave overnight. The curse was like a constant shoulder devil, and it wasn't fair. Why couldn't she have a shoulder angel, too?

Because there's nothing that works like the curse except for the curse, Lucy thought bitterly.

She headed upstairs to her bedroom and flopped on her bed, kicking her shoes off and staring angrily at the ceiling.

I'm such a coward, she thought furiously. *A total coward.*

Maybe the curse would be helpful for something. Maybe she just had to wait until it changed her. She rolled over to tug her phone out of her pocket, turned on the screen, and asked Google, *Are Virgos brave?*

The results made her jaw drop in horror.

They're known for being cowards?!?!

She sat bolt upright, teeth clenched. She slammed her phone on the bedspread.

So it might not be her who was the coward. It might be Virgo acting through her.

She was not going to let it win!

She grabbed her phone and started a text to Billy. Maybe over the phone wasn't ideal, but she had to tell him somehow. But what should she say?

She could use words like *curse* or *zodiac* or *Virgo* when typing things into Google, but she couldn't type them to show to a human. She couldn't tell Billy that she had a power or be specific about how it worked, either.

She could always ask her parents to write an explanation for her and send it, but that seemed way too impersonal. Making your parents do something for you that you were scared to do yourself was cowardly, anyway.

Lucy drummed her fingers on her bed, trying to figure out how to make the meaning obvious despite all her limitations.

I've got a thingy that's bad and does stuff I can't control and I know it's affected you too, she typed in.

Lucy's finger hovered over the "send" button as she read it over. *That makes sense, right?* she tried to convince herself. *Right?*

She groaned and deleted it. No, it didn't. It was complete nonsense. Only somebody who knew about the curses would have any chance of decoding it.

Maybe he does know about the curses! Lucy thought hopefully, sitting up straight. *Maybe he's one of the unknown cursed people, and he has a curse with personality traits that wouldn't make it dangerous for him to be around me! Maybe they ALL are!*

That would be amazing. Then she wouldn't have to explain anything, and they'd all be fine with it, and being with a guy who knew what she was going through would be the best thing ever.

But, well . . .

Lucy sighed. *That's a stupid thing to hope.*

First of all, she didn't actually want any of the guys she liked to have a curse that would make them die early.

Second, if any of the lost zodiac curses had stayed in town or wandered back into it, the families who knew about the curses would have noticed them long ago. The five unknown people with a zodiac curse had to be scattered randomly across the country, maybe across the world.

Third, it wasn't a good idea for two cursed families to mix.

And fourth, how stupid was she? Hellllllo! She didn't want a boyfriend who was going to lose his personality to a curse! That was why she'd made herself stop liking Xander in the first place!

Well, no . . . she'd mostly done it for his own sake. But there was also the teensy tiny selfish fact that she didn't want to date a guy whose original personality was the same as Alex's, because come on, *Alex?* Did he even *have* a personality? The guy was as boring as dirt!

Lucy grinned wryly. Of course, if she said any of that to Pablo, he would tease her by quoting something from the Bible about the importance of being nice to people and not judging them or whatever, because it turned out he was way more religious than he looked at first glance, but since it was better for everybody if she kept disliking Alex and Xander and wasn't charitable to them at all, she would keep on being rude to them in her head, thanks very much.

She looked down at her phone, which still had nothing useful typed in, and groaned. *I'm procrastinating, aren't I?*

See, this was exactly why the curse was such a pain in the neck. She couldn't just explain without having to thinking about it, and she couldn't think about it without letting her mind wander, and she couldn't afford to let her mind wander because that would give the curse more time to turn her into a coward.

She wanted to get it over with, and she wanted to be brave, but she couldn't seem to figure out how to make those happen.

I need a shoulder angel! Lucy thought with frustration. *I need something that will turn me into the kind of person I want to be, not what the curse wants me to become!*

But it was impossible. There was nothing that worked the same way as the curse. Nothing except . . .

Lucy gasped and leapt off her bed. She ran downstairs.

"Mom! Dad! Can I borrow the car? I want to visit Aaron at the hospital!"

Nothing except the current power of the Aries curse.

Chapter 7
Not Quite Wrong

Aaron was asleep when Lucy entered his room, and the lights were out. She should have realized he would be; it was almost eight thirty, and old people always seemed to go to bed early.

She stood there awkwardly, fidgeting, wondering if she should wake him up. Visiting hours ended at nine pm, so she'd thought she'd be okay, and she really, really wanted to talk to him about this right now, but if he was asleep . . .

She moved forward, wanting to check if he was really asleep or if he was just getting ready to fall asleep, because if he wasn't quite asleep yet it would be okay to wake him up, and tripped over one of her undone shoelaces. She stumbled and fell forward, her elbow whacking the bedside table with a hard thump.

"OWWW!" Lucy yelled, grabbing her elbow.

Aaron's eyes slowly opened. "Hello?" he asked groggily.

"Um. Hi," Lucy said sheepishly. This wasn't quite how she'd wanted to start the conversation, but it would do. "It's me, Lucy. Um, are you awake enough to talk? I, um, I wanted to ask you something."

"Mmm. Sure." Aaron sat up slowly and creakily, turning on the lamp at the table beside his bed. The lamp was crooked from Lucy jostling the table when she'd whacked her elbow on it. "What is it, Lucy?"

"Um. Um. Um." Lucy's mind raced. How could she put this in a way that wouldn't make him say no?

She wished she had his power to convince people. Well, no, she didn't. Wait, yes, she did, because then she could use it on herself and all of her problems would be solved.

"Remember you asked if you could do anything to help me, and to just let you know?" Lucy blurted out.

"Yes," Aaron murmured, rubbing his eyes and trying to stifle a yawn. "Did you think of something?"

"Yes!" Lucy said rapidly. "I want a shoulder angel."

Aaron stared at her with mystification written across the lines of his face.

"So, you know the bad thing we both have?" Lucy asked.

"The word we can't say. Yes."

"And you know how it works?"

"I daresay I do," Aaron said dryly.

"Well, *your talent* works the same way. Right? I mean, when you use it on someone, it's basically exactly the same thing."

Aaron stiffened. He didn't answer, and seemed wary.

"But that's a good thing!" Lucy added excitedly. "Because it can be used in a good way!"

"No, it cannot," Aaron said, his voice a hoarse whisper.

"Yes, it can!" Lucy said. "Because it works the same way as the other thing, it could be a *cure!*"

Aaron was silent for a long, long moment.

"I think," he said, very slowly and quietly, "that you're wrong about that. The other thing is much too devious for a brute force approach to work as a cure."

"Oh." Lucy wilted slightly. But she rallied. "Well, then it'll work as a treatment for the symptoms! I mean, when I have a cold, y'know what's making me miserable? The symptoms! So cough medicine's enough to make a difference!"

"Yes . . . pain medicine's helpful, too." Aaron frowned. "But pain medicine can be dangerous."

"So are knives," Lucy said. "But you can't cut up food without them."

"I don't want to mess with your head."

"I don't want you to mess with my head, either. I want to fix my own head, and I want to use the thing you can do as a tool."

"Two wrongs don't make a right."

"They do when the two wrongs are opposites and the right thing is somewhere in between."

Aaron stared at her, pondering.

"What exactly are you asking me to do?" he asked finally.

Hurray! Lucy dug into her pocket for two pieces of paper she had hastily scribbled on while waiting for the elevator downstairs.

"This is the bad list," Lucy said, handing the first paper to him. At the top, the paper said BAD in all caps, underlined several times. "These are the personality traits I want you to convince me to avoid. They're stuff the bad thing in my head is trying to make me become that I don't want."

"I see." Aaron squinted at the paper. "It's a good thing my handwriting is worse than yours, or I'd have trouble making this out. Let's see. 'Organized. Obsessed with spreadsheets. Good at math.'" He blinked and reread it. "'Good at math'? Really?"

"Yup. I hate math, and I reject its having a place in my life entirely."

"You might regret that later in life."

"No, because hating math'll help me *have* a 'later in life.'"

Aaron gave her a bemused look. "That's . . . one perspective, I suppose. Do you have a good list?"

"Yes," Lucy said, pulling the other list out of her pocket. It tore slightly, so she flattened it with care before handing it over. "These are the traits I want you to convince me to develop over time. Not immediately, but, y'know, gradually. Some of them are traits the bad thing wants me to have, but I want them anyway. The rest are ones the bad thing wants me to lose or not gain in the first place, so I want them even more."

"This is a long list," Aaron said, his eyebrows raising.

"Yeah, there are lots of things."

"'Affectionate. Loving. Loyal,'" Aaron read. "'Honest. Brave. Impossible to intimidate. Clingy.'" He paused. "'Clingy'? This is on the good list?"

"Yeah, clingy's part of who my dad is, and he wouldn't be himself without it."

Aaron stopped. "Are these all describing your dad?"

"Yup."

"I thought you were modeling yourself after an abstract concept."

"I've never met any abstract concepts."

"I see . . ." Aaron read through the rest silently. At last, he set the two papers in front of him. "Well, theoretically, I don't see any reason why this wouldn't work."

"Yesssss!" Lucy cried, pumping her fist.

"But that's a *theory*," Aaron stressed. "That doesn't mean there won't be any unpredictable negative consequences that can't be fixed. I've never tried anything like this before. It could be a huge risk."

"Risks are okay," Lucy said. "Much better than a guaranteed bad thing."

Aaron tapped his fingers on the papers, seeming hesitant to get started. "Do your parents know about this?"

"No, because it's none of their business."

"What if something goes wrong?"

"Then it's my fault, not yours. If I turn into a braindead zombie or something, you can tell them if you want to, but I'd rather you didn't because it's none of their business and they shouldn't blame you. Anyway, I don't think anything bad is going to happen, so. Y'know." Lucy took a deep breath. "Can we get started? I think visiting hours are going to end soon."

Aaron glanced at the watch on his wrist. "What time do they end?"

"Nine o'clock."

"That's five minutes from now."

"Then let's get started now! Pleeeeeeeease?"

Aaron hesitated. "Are you really sure you've thought this through?"

"I've thought it through enough, and I don't want to go home tonight without a shoulder angel, because you might die tonight, and then where would I be?!"

Aaron put a hand to his face and laughed wryly. "I notice 'tact' was on neither of those lists, so I hope you develop it eventually . . . but you do have a point. Okay, Lucy. Okay."

Lucy cheered silently.

Chapter 8
Not Quite Time

"No!" Lucy said in frustration, slamming her phone down on her bed.

She was back from seeing Aaron, and she couldn't tell if his persuasion had helped at all, but that was probably a good thing. It was supposed to be subtle and long-term, not instant and obvious, after all. The thing was, she didn't feel especially braver than before, which meant she was right back where she had been an hour ago.

I have to do it now, Lucy thought with grim determination. *I have to do it now, so that I don't chicken out.*

But she wasn't any smarter than she'd been an hour ago, either, and she was finding that no explanation would come that made sense and didn't sound vague and meaningless.

Okay, fine. I'll have to do it in person. I can play charades. Or use crossword puzzle-like hints. If I do it with all four at once, one of them's bound to guess correctly, and then I can say "yes" and move on until they get the whole thing.

That seemed so, so, so stupid, though.

Not Quite Time

Of course, maybe she just thought it was a stupid idea because she was looking for excuses to procrastinate it further.

Rashly, Lucy grabbed her phone and typed in, *Come to my house at four pm tomorrow! I'm going to tell you my big secret. Here's a hint: five-letter word, rhyming with "purse." Come with your best guess what it is!*

Then she added a dozen winky faces and pushed the button to send it to all four of the guys at once.

Lucy dropped her phone and breathed a sigh of relief.

There. It was done. She hadn't told them all yet, but the time was coming, and it was soon. And she couldn't possibly chicken out, because there was no good way to explain away that hint without telling the truth.

She had eighteen hours left to figure out how to do that.

♏

Lucy spent all morning ignoring her classes and scribbling down possible explanations in her notebook, none of which made any sense when she reread them. It was frustrating. She was starting to think it really wasn't possible to explain things on her own.

Yes, there was charades, but did she really *have* to play charades? What if none of them guessed the right words? It wasn't exactly a normal thing she was trying to explain.

Maybe she should ask her mom or dad to give the explanation for her. But no . . . no . . . no . . . nooooooooooo . . .

Finally, listening to the bell ring to end math class as she scribbled out her fifth terrible attempt, she looked up and saw the guy in front of her stand up. A brainwave came to her.

"You can do it!" Lucy exclaimed.

Alex gave her a blank look. "Ex . . . cuse me?"

"You can explain things," Lucy gabbled all in one breath. "Because you're not what I am, but you know what it's like, and you also know what it's like to be under my, you know, what I can do. Can you tell some people how the thing works?!"

Alex's face held no expression.

"Please?!" Lucy pleaded.

"Why?" Alex asked flatly.

"It — it's for four guys I like," Lucy said in a rush. "'Cause I don't want to keep using it on them without their permission, but I can't ask their permission if they don't know, and I can't tell them myself, and nobody else would do it right. Mom would try to make me sound completely blameless, Caleb would badmouth me, and my dad — well, actually, I dunno what my dad would do, but there's no way he's unbiased on the subject of me dating. He's super overprotective. Oh, please!"

Alex stared at her for a long moment. He didn't blink.

"Please, please, please, please?!" Lucy swallowed, her heart pounding, as she pleated her fingers in front of her.

"It's true that I bear you no ill will," Alex said in a slow and measured voice. "And I wish you well in your endeavor. But I have no wish to be recognized as part of it."

"Then write it down!" Lucy cried. "Make it anonymous! I can pull out a piece of paper with an explanation and show it to them, right? The thingamajiggy won't stop me, right?"

"No," Alex said slowly. "As long as the words are mine and not yours, it won't stop you from showing it to other people."

Lucy made a face. "Well, it's not like it'd let me write down anything useful anyway."

"You'd be surprised," Alex said. "You can use any of the words that are normally forbidden as long as they aren't meant for communication with another human being. A journal can be kept freely, for instance."

Lucy stared at him, startled. "Are you sure about that?"

"Yes. My father kept one."

Wow. Lucy's mouth opened. *Guess that would explain why I can type whatever I want into Google. And guess I couldn't ever show someone my search history to help them figure it out. The curse is weird.*

Alex seemed to be pondering.

"All right," he said finally. "As long as you will keep me fully anonymous, I'll write an explanation that you may show to them. I'll put it in your locker in half an hour."

"Oh, you can just write it in my notebook right now," Lucy said, proffering it.

"No," Alex said firmly. "It needs to be typed so that my handwriting cannot be recognized."

Lucy couldn't stop an impatient groan emerging from the back of her throat. Him and his obsession with privacy.

But Alex was as good as his word. When she reached her locker half an hour later, after strolling through a gauntlet of flirting guys emerging from their last classes of the day and making excuses to her friends about why she couldn't hang out this afternoon, she opened her locker door and saw a piece of paper waft out and fall to the ground.

She picked it up and saw exactly the explanation she needed.

To whomever it may concern:

Lucy has a magical power to make boys fall in love with her. It affects both physical attraction and emotions, but seems to work primarily on physical attraction. It is not something she fully has control over, as it is only possible for her to turn it off by not being attracted to the individual.

If she is showing this to you, she probably suspects you've been affected by her power, and she wants you to be aware of it in case that changes your opinion on whether you wish to continue having feelings for her.

Be aware that this is not a power she chose to have. It is an accompaniment to a curse that cannot be broken, will shorten her lifespan, and will change her personality over time. It is a grim curse, and not one she chose.

She cannot explain any of this directly herself, as an inability to speak directly about the curse is another part of the curse.

Please do not share this information with anyone else. Lucy is sharing this with you because she trusts you to be silent and not spread this private information to others. Your absolute discretion is appreciated.

Lucy's lips twitched up into a wry smile. She would've known this was from Alex even if she hadn't asked him to write it. Only he would put such a strong emphasis on the need for privacy, despite the fact that that was something she could say for herself just fine.

Still, she appreciated it. He was a nice guy. Annoyingly quiet, but nice.

She folded the paper into messy halves and quarters, and then shoved it into her jeans pocket, wrinkling the edges as she shoved it in to fit.

Now she was ready.

Now it was time.

Chapter 9
Not Quite Real

When Lucy got home, she found her mom outside weeding the garden, pulled the note out of her pocket, showed it to her, and said that four of her guys were coming over so Lucy could show this to them and maybe pick one of them as a real boyfriend, so could Mom pleeeeeeeeeeeeease take Dad out of the house for awhile?

Fortunately, Lucy's mother understood immediately why it mattered, and it wasn't long before she was dragging her husband out of the house with the announcement that they hadn't been on a real date in almost a week, and she was tired of her teenage daughter dating more often than they were.

"There's a solution to that," Lucy's dad grumbled as his wife shoved him out the front door. "Lucy could go on a few less —"

The door shut behind them.

Lucy buried her face in a pillow from the sofa and giggled.

The first of the guys arrived only ten minutes later.

"Verse?" Pablo asked as he came in the door.

"Nope!" Lucy said. "But good guessing!"

"Do I get a second hint now?"

"Not till everyone's here!"

George was the next to arrive.

"Have you guessed the secret word?" Lucy asked teasingly.

"Huh?" George looked befuddled for a moment. "Oh. Right. What was the clue again?"

"Five-letter word, rhyming with 'purse.'"

"Reverse?" he hazarded.

"That's not five letters!"

"Sorry, I'm not very good at crossword puzzles."

Billy was next, and Jonas arrived soon afterwards. Billy guessed "nurse," and Jonas guessed "worse."

It's a good thing I didn't decide to go with clues and charades, Lucy thought, exasperated.

"Okay," she said with a bright smile, pulling the well-crumpled paper out of her pocket. Her heart was pounding, and her hands shook slightly. "Well, here's my secret! I — I can't read it to you, so, um . . . I'll put it on the table, and you can all read it together!"

She darted to the coffee table, unfolded the paper, and laid it out so they could see it. Pablo and Jonas got up from their seats to move closer, while George and Billy leaned forward to read.

George finished it first. "Is this a joke?" he asked.

Lucy's mouth went dry. She tried to summon a teasing smile, and failed. Instead, she just shook her head.

Jonas finished next. "That's, uh . . . wow."

Lucy nodded, fidgeting nervously.

Billy finished slowly, mouthing the words. He merely looked up in puzzlement, as if he still didn't understand.

Pablo was last. His face was ashen when he finished.

Lucy's heart accelerated into panic mode.

"So . . . this is *true?*" George said, pointing at the paper.

"Yes," Lucy whispered. "It is. It's — well, it says there why I want you to know."

She found herself grateful that Alex had slightly overexplained. Even though the curse wouldn't have blocked her from saying her reason for telling them, the words stuck in her throat anyway.

"Well," George said with an awkward laugh. "Well. I guess that doesn't really matter. I mean, the curse sounds bad, but the power — it doesn't really matter if my feelings are real or fake."

Lucy breathed out. "Really?"

"Sure." George shrugged.

"Yours are probably real, anyway," Lucy blurted out. "You've liked me for over a year, and this started three months ago."

"Oh, really?" George looked pleased. "Cool."

"Huhhhhh . . ." Jonas muttered, rereading the note.

Lucy swallowed. "Yes?"

"Three months ago, huh?"

"Yeah," she said in a small voice.

"Okay. I'm out." He stood up. "That's when I started thinking you were hot. I dunno why he's okay with it, but I'm not. Turn it off or whatever you do, okay?"

Lucy felt sick to her stomach. "It — it might take awhile. I have to stop liking you."

"Okay. Then do it." Jonas walked over to her and patted her on the shoulder. "Sorry, Luce. You're nice. You're fun to hang out with. But I'm not good with this. I'm gonna go, and you talk with them. It's probably best if we avoid each other from now on."

Lucy nodded, a huge lump in her throat.

After Jonas left, Billy, George, and Pablo all stayed silent. George was watching the other two. Pablo had his face in his hands, and his shoulders were tense. Billy just kept looking baffled.

"B-Billy?" Lucy prodded nervously. "What do you think?"

"Ummmm . . ." Billy looked down at the paper and then back up again. "I don't think I get it."

"It's what it says!" Lucy said, trying not to get angry.

"Yeah, but magic doesn't exist."

"Yes, it *does!*" Lucy shouted. "Are you an idiot?!"

Billy stood up, looking huffy. "I don't wanna date someone who thinks I'm an idiot."

Lucy's throat tightened. "I'm sorry. I didn't mean —"

"I mean, what kind of sick joke are you playing?"

Lucy stopped. She stared at him.

"You're right," she said finally. "I do think you're an idiot."

"Well, bye then," Billy said with irritation, stalking to the front door and walking out. He slammed it behind him.

That just left Pablo.

Who was being very, very silent and seemed very upset.

Lucy's fists clenched and unclenched as swirls of panic spiraled through her.

You've still got George, she tried to tell herself. *No matter what, he's okay.*

But it *wasn't* okay if she wound up with George! She wanted *Pablo* to choose her! She'd been trying to convince herself she'd be okay with any of them, but she wouldn't, and it had to be him, and what if he said no?!

At last, after what seemed like an eternity but was probably only about twenty minutes of silence, Pablo looked up.

"Can I talk with you in private?" he asked in a low voice.

Lucy's heart raced. She looked over at George.

"Sure," he said gently.

She took Pablo to the laundry room, which doubled as the downstairs bathroom, and shut the door.

Even then, he was silent. He looked like he was about to cry.

"You don't want me, do you?" Lucy said in a broken voice. "That's why I was afraid to tell you. I thought you'd say no."

"To what?" Pablo mumbled.

Lucy fidgeted and looked at her hands. "To being my boyfriend because I love you and I couldn't ask you unless you knew the truth and now that you know it, you don't want me!"

Her voice got rather loud at the end.

Pablo stared at her in astonishment. "You . . . you were going to ask me . . .?"

"Yeah, because you're *awesome!*" Lucy exclaimed. "You're everything I've ever wanted in a boyfriend!"

"You're everything I've ever wanted, too," he whispered.

Lucy's eyes widened with hope. "Really?"

"Yeah, but . . . I don't think you want me." He looked away, his eyes fixed on the washer and dryer. "Because I'm gay."

Lucy's mouth sagged open. ". . . What? That's impossible."

"I sure wish it were."

"But you've never shown any sign of it!"

"Yeah! Because I don't want to be! I prayed for years that I'd find a girl I could fall in love with, and then I finally did, and now I find out it's *fake!*" His voice broke at the end.

Lucy swallowed. "So you don't want to be in love with me?" she asked in a small voice.

"What?" Pablo gave her an incredulous look. "Of course I do! I'd rather not live a celibate life, I just thought it was the only way to be faithful to God if I never found a girl I wanted to m— never mind — and then I did, and now it turns out it's *fake!*"

He looked like he was about to cry.

Lucy took a deep breath. She was still recovering from the shock. But . . . really, one thing was obvious. "Who says it's fake?"

Pablo didn't look at her. "The timeframe —"

"No! I didn't ask if it was caused by the thingamajiggy I have, because clearly it was. I asked if it's fake! If you want to be in love with me, and you *are* in love with me, and I want to be in love with you, and I *am* in love with you, then that means it's real. Q.E.D.!"

Pablo stared at her for a moment. Then his shoulders started to shake. She was worried for a second, and then she realized he was laughing. "I don't think you know what 'Q.E.D.' means."

"It means 'I totally proved it,' right?"

Pablo was laughing openly now. "Well, yes, but . . ."

"There we go!" she said triumphantly.

"What I'm saying is, I'm not sure your logic is sound!"

"Psshhhh!" She waved her hand. "I don't care about logic. I care about choice. Do you choose me?"

He was silent for a moment. Then he took a deep breath.

He walked over and took her hand.

"Yes," he said. "Yes, I do."

Chapter 10
Not Quite Done

George was waiting for them in the living room when they left the laundry room together, hand-in-hand. She'd almost forgotten he was still there.

"Um," Lucy said awkwardly. "Um . . . hi, George. So . . . Pablo and I talked, and we're kind of sort of thinking that I'm going to be exclusive with him from now on . . . ."

George sighed. "Yes, I kind of thought that was the direction this was going."

Lucy swallowed. "Sorry."

George shrugged, stood, and shook Pablo's hand. "Well, I'm happy for you. Wish it'd been me, but that's how it goes."

Lucy felt like a heel. George was a way nicer person than she would be. "Can we still be friends?" she asked hopefully.

"I hope so." George took her hand and shook it. "Your secret's safe with me, of course. I'm going to stop being a third wheel now. I'll see you both at school."

He left, shutting the front door softly behind him.

Lucy put a hand to her forehead and groaned.

"Any regrets?" Pablo said with a teasing smile, but his voice sounded a little worried.

"Nope!" Lucy said, kissing him on the lips.

She pulled back and hesitated for a second, then decided she should probably tell him.

"To be honest, Pablo . . . George was my second choice, but only because I really like him and respect him. I don't think I've had feelings for him for a long time. Which in a way might be a good thing because it means his feelings are probably entirely natural these days, but it's also a really bad thing, because, well, I'd rather have a guy I'm attracted to."

Pablo was silent for a moment. "What about the reverse?"

Lucy frowned. "What do you mean?"

"Well," Pablo said, "if your curse ever breaks and your power disappears . . ."

"Not gonna happen. It's impossible."

"It's better not to assume. So, think about it: if your curse ever breaks and your power disappears, that'll put me right back where I was before we met."

Lucy went silent.

"So — are you okay with me still wanting to be with you even if I'm not attracted to you anymore?"

Lucy swallowed. "That . . . sounds much less fun," she said in a small voice.

"I completely agree." He touched the side of her face. "But if our relationship is based on the assumption that your power will be there to make things easier forever, it's much too fragile."

Lucy hesitated. "Well, what would *you* do?"

"I've already chosen," he said. "You asked me if I chose you, and I said yes. I meant that with or without your power."

Lucy scrunched up her face. "Well, if we, say, got married — which I'm so not ready to do right now! — and it went away and you weren't in love with me anymore, where would that leave us?"

He shrugged. "You'd be my best friend and the only person I'd want to spend the rest of my life with."

"That doesn't sound nearly as romantic!" she complained.

He laughed. "No, it doesn't, does it? But a lot of marriage relationships *do* go that way, you know. It's very common, and that doesn't mean it's right to end them. I don't believe in divorce. If we ever get married, I'm staying no matter what, unless you ask me to leave." He grew serious. "So, if we ever got married, would you take it as seriously as I would? Because if you wouldn't . . . that's a dealbreaker for me."

Lucy licked her lips. "You're not, like . . . asking me to marry you right now, are you?"

"Oh, no!" Pablo burst out laughing. "For one thing, I'm not giving my family that kind of satisfaction!"

"Good, because . . . I'm so not ready for that! As for your question, um . . . give me a minute to think about it."

Lucy sat down on the couch and thought for several minutes. It was a hard question. But she decided he was right: if he was willing to devote his life to her, she had to be willing to do the same. They didn't have to make the decision of whether they were going to right now, but they did have to make the decision of whether they would see it through if they did.

Pablo sat down next to her, his face questioning.

"Okay," Lucy said at last. "If we ever reach the point that we want to get married, and you lose your feelings for me afterwards, I won't complain about it, and I'll stay."

Pablo touched her face and smiled. "*That's* what makes it real."

Lucy got up, grinned, and flopped on his lap.

"Oof!" Pablo said. "You're a little heavy."

"That's okay," Lucy said coyly, playing with his hair.

"Says the girl who doesn't have a hundred pounds of weight on her lap."

"One twenty, and thanks for the compliment."

"I'm serious! You're heavy!"

"Just *try* to get me off."

"Oh, in *that* case . . .!" He stood up, dumped her on the couch, and then sat on top of her.

Lucy shrieked with laughter. "You're way heavier! Get off!"

"Nope, I'm going to sit here for as long as you sat on me."

So naturally she had to tickle him.

About ten minutes later, they settled the battle by having her lie on the couch with her head on his lap while she flipped through the channels on TV, looking for anything good on.

"Hey, Pablo?" Lucy asked, looking up at his face from his lap. "I've got a weird question for you. Are there any advantages to you in being gay?"

He paused. "Excuse me?"

"I'm just wondering. Because it's not like it's going to go away. I mean, you're gonna be attracted to guys for the rest of your life, whether or not you have feelings for me. But I've just learned there's an advantage to my thingy —"

"Your curse?"

"Yeah."

"What's the advantage?"

"You, duh!"

"I said I'd stick around even without it."

"Yeah, but would you have ever considered me in the first place without it?"

Pablo pondered. "Probably not," he admitted.

"See? There's an advantage to me. So I'm wondering if there's an advantage to you in the thing *you* have that you don't want."

Pablo ran his fingers through Lucy's hair for awhile. "You know," he said at last, in a surprised voice, "I think there may be."

"Really?" she asked.

He nodded. "Before I figured out I was gay, I didn't really take my religion that seriously. I was kind of like you. I didn't really see a reason to bother with it. But once I figured out I was gay, the question of whether I believed in my religion became of crucial importance. So I did a lot of studying, a lot of praying, and a lot of thinking about it, and I determined I did. I think that made me a much better person."

"Huh." Lucy cocked her head to the side. "So is this a subtle hint that I should start, like, attending mass more often?"

He laughed. "I'm not gonna make you, but it would certainly be nice if you did."

"Okay, fine. But only if you're going with me, because then it can be like a date. A really, really, really boring date, because I assume you won't be kissing me in a church."

"I could kiss you right now," Pablo said with a grin.

"Ooh! Good idea!" Lucy got up and bounced onto his lap.

"Lucyyyyyy! You're heavy!"

"Kiss me anyway."

So he did.

"WHAT IS THIS?" a voice roared from behind them.

She spun around and saw her dad standing in the doorway, crimson-faced. Behind him was her mom, looking amused.

Lucy coughed and scooted away from her boyfriend. "Oh, hi, Dad. We've been watching TV."

"Only watching TV?!" he growled.

"All right, and kissing, too." Lucy gave him a wicked smile. "Pablo's a great kisser, and he's going to be really fun to have as a boyfriend. Want me to describe what I like about his kissing?"

Her dad's eyes looked like they were about to bulge out of his head.

"Harry," Lucy's mom said, obviously trying not to smile.

"Don't 'Harry' me!" he roared, glaring at Lucy. "You can't invite a boy over here without supervision! You know the rules! And that goes double for a boyfriend! And as for him *being* your boyfriend, you need my permission for that!"

"No, I don't."

"Yes, you do!"

"No, I don't."

"Yes, you do!"

"Sir, 'the victorious strategist only seeks battle after the victory has already been won,'" Pablo said with an impish grin. "Sun Tzu."

Lucy's father was speechless for a moment. Then he sighed and said, "Oh, all right, he'll do."

www.ingramcontent.com/pod-product-compliance
Lightning Source LLC
Chambersburg PA
CBHW022122050726
47591CB00002B/895